YOU ARE AMAZING

GIRL

Megan Donovan

Content

The Field Trip

It was just before twelve, and the school day was about to end. Lena could no longer wait patiently in her seat. She had had a great day. She had learned well and enjoyed the breaks with her best friend. Still, Lena felt excited to go home and share lunch with her family. Afterward, tired from a long school day, she would rest in her room.

Before the bell rang, Lena's homeroom teacher, Mrs. King, smiled and announced, "Children, I have great news! In two weeks, we're going on a school trip! We'll be away for a whole week!"

A loud buzz of voices erupted in the classroom—joy mingled with dread and disappointment:
"Oh no, I don't feel like it!" sulked Tina, sitting to the left of Lena. Julia, on the other hand, seemed visibly delighted. She called out, "Where are we going, Mrs. King?"

The uproar in the classroom meant Mrs. King almost had to shout to make herself heard. Lena waited anxiously for her teacher's answer and could already feel the stress rising in her. Still, she stared at Mrs. King in silence.

"We're going to summer camp!" she replied.

The children looked at each other and whispered, "What's that? Summer camp?" Only a few seemed to know what Mrs. King meant.

She explained, "At summer camp, you can do lots of fun activities like climbing, sailing, or playing table tennis. It's a place where children can burn off energy. And we'll all go together and stay for a whole week!"

The commotion picked up again. Some students cheered and looked forward to going to camp.

Others sighed. "Oh no, I don't want to go sailing," Tina said, tears in her eyes. Lena found it strange that Tina had only remembered the word "sailing" from everything the teacher had mentioned. Lena didn't feel like sailing, climbing, or being far away from her parents. Besides, a week seemed like an eternity, and that terrified her.

Lena turned to Tina and shared her disappointment. "I don't feel like it either," she said with a frown.

When the school bell finally rang, Mrs. King said goodbye and gave each child a permission slip. All students had to give it to their parents when they went home.

Without the signed paper, no child could participate in the trip. Lena lowered her eyes and picked up her bag. She grabbed the paper from her desk and walked out of the classroom without a word. She didn't even think to say goodbye to the teacher. Lost in thought, she simply walked away.

Alone, she went home. She was seven years old, already tall, and her house was nearby. On her way home, a thousand thoughts flashed through her mind.

"If Mom and Dad don't sign the paper, I can't go. All I have to do is not tell them, and when they leave for the trip, I can stay home!" she thought. But that would be a lie, and Lena didn't want to lie. Lying wasn't right, as her parents had explained many times. So, what was she supposed to do?

When she arrived, Dad greeted her warmly. "Ah, my angel, you're home! How was your day?" he asked with a smile.

Lena was so happy to be home and see her parents again that she forgot about the permission slip. Looking at her parents, she grinned from ear to ear and replied, "Good! I played hide and seek with Julia and Tina, and I won!" Then, she sat at the table and ate the spaghetti her dad had cooked.

She was about to have seconds when her dad asked, "Don't you have something we need to sign?"

Lena froze. "Does he know?" she wondered. "No, he can't. The teacher only told us about it today, so he can't possibly know!"

Lena's mind raced. A few seconds passed, but she still hadn't answered her father. Surprised, Dad asked again, this time in a more serious voice, "Lena? Do you have papers for Mom and me?"

Lena hesitated. She remembered her earlier thoughts. No, she didn't want to lie. Her parents would be too disappointed if she did. Lena already knew lying was wrong. Although it took a lot of effort, she preferred to tell the truth.

So, she finally answered with a grin, "Yes, I got a permission slip for a trip to summer camp!"

Dad replied, "That's nice! Please give it to me so I can take a look and sign it."

Lena began to cry when she heard these words.

Immediately, Dad asked worriedly, "What's wrong, sweetheart? Why are you crying? You know, if you got a bad grade, it's not the end of the world!"

"No, I didn't get a bad grade. It's something else that makes me sad," Lena replied, still crying. She stood up and took the permission slip out of her folder.

"I don't want you to sign this paper!" she continued, sobbing as tears dripped down her cheeks.

Dad took a quick look at the paper and immediately understood. He tried to reassure her. "You know, Lena, when I was your age, I also went to summer camp with my class. I was scared to go without my parents," he began quietly. Lena calmed down a little. Dad had her full attention.

"I was really scared, and the trip was long. I even cried because I missed my parents, my room, and my toys!" her father continued. Lena looked at him with astonished eyes. Her dad had cried? She couldn't imagine that.

Dad lovingly stroked her cheek and continued, "I cried a lot on the trip, and you know what? I cried on the way back, too!"

On the way back, too? Lena didn't understand; why would Dad cry on the way home?

Seeing her confusion, Dad smiled and explained, "I had so much fun at camp, and I spent so much time with my friends and teachers that I didn't want to leave. I didn't want to go home!"

Surprised, Lena raised her eyebrows. "Impossible," she thought. She couldn't believe it. How could anyone be happy being away from their parents and home?

Dad spoke again. "I'm sure you'll have a great time, too! You'll have fun, make lots of memories, and learn new things!

And when you're on the bus ride home, you might even be sad to leave."

Lena didn't answer, but she wasn't crying anymore. She thought about what her dad had said. Dad was glad to see her calm down. He hugged her and said, "You know what, my angel? Mom and I will sign your permission slip. I'm sure you'll have a good time with your friends. When you get back, you can tell us all about it! I can't wait to hear about your adventures! And if you like it, we'll go again during our next vacation — just you, me, and Mom!"

"And if I don't like it?" Lena asked softly. "If you don't like it, we'll choose another

place to go on vacation together!" Dad
replied.

After talking with her father, Lena forgot
her worries. When her mother came
home, Lena said, beaming with joy,
"Mom, Mom! Guess what? I'm going to
summer camp with my class! I'll be away
for a whole week!"

Mom didn't understand everything at
first. She glanced at Dad, then at Lena's
shining face. She grinned widely at Lena
and congratulated her. "You're getting
so big! You're going to school on your
own, and now you're going on a class trip
without us. That's a big step! I'm proud of
you!" she said, pressing a kiss on Lena's
forehead.

Although Lena still had some doubts and fears, Mom's words put her mind at ease.

Two weeks later, Lena took the bus to the countryside with Mrs. King and the whole class. Mom and Dad were right: she cried a little during the ride. She didn't know what to expect at camp, which scared her a bit. She also missed her parents.

On the first day, she forgot all her worries. She had more fun than ever before. On the way back, she cried again—this time because the trip was over, and she'd have to return to everyday life. She wasn't the only one; Tina had wept on the bus, too.

Lena dried her tears, thinking of Dad's promise to go back to the camp next vacation. She could hardly wait. What a wonderful week it had been!

The Big, Bad Bully

This morning, Laura didn't want to get out of bed. The alarm clock had been ringing for a while, but Laura turned it off. She wrapped herself in her comforter and turned to face the wall. Today, she would rather sleep in and stay in bed. Outside, the rain poured, and the air felt freezing.

Her mom had been up preparing breakfast and packing Laura's things. When she saw the clock ticking and Laura still wasn't there, she began to worry.

"What is she doing? Didn't her alarm go off?" Mom scolded quietly so as not to wake the rest of the family.

She went to Laura's room, but she saw no light and heard no sound to indicate Laura was awake.

She knocked softly and whispered, "Laura?" There was no answer. Then she cracked the door open and tried again, "Laura?" Still no sound. This time, Mom grew impatient.

She opened the door wider and took large steps toward Laura's bed. She gently put her hand on Laura's shoulder and shook her softly.

"Laura, you have to get up or you'll be late. Didn't the alarm go off this morning?"

Laura yawned briefly and tried to go back to sleep, so Mom had no choice but to pull the covers off her.

Laura sat on the edge of the bed. She looked tired but also sad. She said quietly to her mother,

"I'm not hungry. And I don't want to go to school," putting on her pouty face.

Mom, who was about to leave the room,

immediately stopped. What did that mean—she wasn't hungry? What did that mean—she didn't want to go to school?

Laura was now seven years old, and never before had she uttered those words. She had always loved school. She was a curious girl who enjoyed learning and asking questions. Besides, school was where all her friends were!
Mom realized Laura wouldn't suddenly stop wanting to go to school unless something bad had happened.

So, Mom came back and sat down next to Laura on the edge of the bed. She put her arm around her daughter's shoulders and asked, "You're not hungry? Really?"

Laura said nothing and nodded.

"Then, can I eat your piece of chocolate cake for breakfast?"

Laura raised her head and looked at her mother.

Chocolate cake was her favorite, so maybe she could eat a piece after all. She didn't have the strength to answer, but Mom understood and smiled at her.

Mom asked the most important question: "Why don't you want to go to school today? You normally like it a lot. Did something happen?"

Laura put on her sad face again and

didn't answer right away. She hesitated.
She didn't know how to explain.

She thought back to the last few weeks. She thought about the tall boy who constantly teased her in the schoolyard. She thought of the times when he pushed her, took her ball, and even snatched her hair ties. He would hold her hair ties in his hand and stretch his arm up in the air, saying,

"Come on, come get your hair ties!" while laughing loudly.

Laura was so small next to him that even when she jumped as high as she could, she still couldn't reach her hair ties. He said mean things and kept making fun of her.

She felt humiliated and didn't know how to explain her feelings. She was ashamed on one hand, but angry on the other. After all, it wasn't fair.

Why should this boy tease her? She hadn't done anything to him! She didn't even know him. So why would he do that? What was she supposed to tell her mom?

"If Mom knew, she might think I did something mean and the boy is just getting revenge," thought Laura. "Or she might think I'm just pathetic because I can't defend myself. What if Mom thinks the same thing the boy does? That I'm small, pathetic, and stupid? What if Mom stops loving me because of him?"

Laura's thoughts were in turmoil, and soon her emotions were, too. She didn't know what to say or do, and tears started to roll down her cheeks.

Mom was surprised by her reaction but also concerned. She hurriedly took Laura in her arms, stroking her back gently. "It's going to be okay; it's going to be okay," she repeated, though she didn't yet know what was wrong with her daughter.

She waited until Laura calmed down and then asked,
"Can you tell me what happened, sweetheart? Why are you so sad about going to school?"
Laura answered through her sobs,

"There's this big bully boy who always teases me!"

Mom stayed with Laura for a long time, asking questions to truly understand the situation. When Laura realized that Mom was really listening, she felt a sense of relief and began to spill everything on her mind. Surprisingly, it felt good to talk about it. And Mom didn't seem to like her any less, as Laura had feared. After their conversation, Mom even said,
"It's not your fault, and I understand how you feel. It's not fair for him to tease you. Come on, let's have breakfast. We'll go to school together, and I'll talk to your teacher and his, too!"

Laura didn't like Mom's idea at all. She was afraid of being seen as a "tattle-tale." If word got out, Laura feared she would be rejected by all the kids at school. Still, she decided to trust Mom.

Laura's crying had woken Dad up, too. He had come to see what was wrong because he was worried about his daughter. He had overheard what Laura confided in her mother, so he chose not to intervene just yet, fearing Laura wouldn't want to talk if he interrupted.

When Mom left Laura's room, she saw Dad waiting outside the door. She stepped aside, and Laura saw her father. He said to her,

"I'm going to wake up your little brother, and we'll all have breakfast together. Then we'll go to school with you!" He hugged Laura, gave her a big kiss, and praised her for talking to Mom. He told her how important it was to talk about her problems, as that was the only way they could help her.

Time flew by. They hurried through breakfast, washed up, dressed, packed, and headed

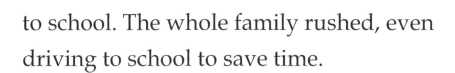

to school. The whole family rushed, even driving to school to save time.

When they arrived, many parents and children were standing in front of the school. Laura and her parents had arrived just on time. They all got out of the car and walked to the front gate where the teachers were waiting for their students.

Dad leaned toward Laura and whispered, "Here's the plan. You'll join your friends as usual, go to class like you always do, and have a wonderful day."
Hearing these words made Laura feel nervous again, but Dad wasn't done.
"In the meantime, we'll talk to your teacher, the bully's teacher, and maybe even the bully's parents. If he bothers you again today, tell your teacher right away."

Laura replied with a sad look,
"If I do that, they'll call me a tattle-tale..."

Mom interrupted, "It doesn't mean you're
a tattle-tale if you talk about your feelings.
If someone hurts you, you have to speak
up. That's the most important thing.
That's how we can help you!"

Laura felt reassured. She went to school
and met her friends, who were already
eagerly waiting for her. She didn't
know what Mom and Dad had told her
homeroom teacher, Mrs. Archer, or what
the boy had said. When the bell rang to
start class, Mrs. Archer waved Laura over
and said,
"I talked to your mom and dad. If anyone

bothers you, come and tell me right away. Agreed?"

Laura nodded without saying a word.

During the first recess, the big bully was nowhere to be seen, so she enjoyed herself without fear. This hadn't happened in a long time. Shortly after recess began, Mrs.

Archer waved Laura over again.
"Stay here for a bit, please. We're waiting for someone," she said.

Laura didn't understand. Who were they waiting for? A short time later, the bully arrived with his teacher. Laura felt her heart pounding faster and faster.

The boy's teacher, Mrs. Mantel, began to speak.
"Don't worry, everything's fine. Tim has something to say to you. We had a long talk earlier, and I think he understands now."

Tim! So that was the bully's name. Laura couldn't look him in the face, but he wouldn't look at her either. Tim stared at the ground.

"Well, Tim?" Mrs. Mantel prompted sternly.

Tim took a deep breath and raised his head, though he still kept his eyes on the floor. He said, "I'm sorry I hurt you. I was just trying to have a little fun. I won't do it again. I promise."

Laura was surprised to hear both an apology and a promise. It was incredible! Mom, Dad, and the teachers had helped her solve the problem. Now she could play with her friends without him teasing her. That was great!
Her face brightened and her anxiety

faded. She finally felt relieved and happy!

Mrs. Archer asked, "Is there anything you want to say to Tim?"
Laura thought for a moment and then said, "Yes. You were very mean to me, even though I didn't do anything to you. That's not fair. I want you to leave me alone from now on."

Tim had already promised not to tease her, but it felt empowering for Laura to say it out loud. She was finally able to express her feelings.
Tim nodded, and Mrs. Archer added, "The teachers and I watch the schoolyard, and now that we know about this, we'll be keeping an eye on you. So stop

misbehaving!" She gave Tim a firm look.

"Good, you can both go play now!" Mrs. Mantel said to conclude the conversation.

The children rushed outside, returning to their friends. Laura finally had peace in the schoolyard. Tim stayed with his friends and played ball instead of teasing others. Laura was satisfied. Her problem had been solved without the other children finding out, and the teachers had been understanding.

Laura learned something important that day: you should never tolerate bullying. You should never accept mean behavior from anyone. And if you need help, don't be afraid to ask for it.

That evening, Laura hugged her parents and thanked them for helping her solve the problem. Without her parents, she would never have told anyone she was unhappy, and she would have continued to be teased by the big bully.

Mom and Dad praised Laura again for trusting them and speaking honestly about her feelings.

Laura was excited to go back to school the next day, and she had gained an incredible amount of self-confidence. From now on, she would listen to herself. If something went wrong, she wouldn't stay silent anymore!

I am
valuable

Soccer

Sophie and Anna were sitting in the schoolyard, overlooking the small soccer field during the day's last break. Only two more hours of classes, and then they could go home. As always, they watched the boys play soccer.

"I'd like to play soccer!" said Sophie, looking longingly at the soccer field. "Me too! That looks really fun!" replied Anna.

They had been watching the soccer games every recess for a few weeks. By watching, they had learned the rules of the game. The previous week, they had finally felt confident enough to play. Full of anticipation, they ran onto the soccer field and asked the boys, "We want to play, too! Which team are we going to be on?"

The boys, however, were not at all enthusiastic. They simply replied, "No, you can't play. Just sit on the bench and cheer us on!" Then they pointed to the bench where Sophie and Anna had sat for several weeks. After that, the boys turned around and resumed playing soccer. How rude!

However, Sophie and Anna were persistent and didn't give up. They stayed on the soccer field a while longer. Then some of the boys started yelling, "Get off the field; you're interrupting the game!"

Since then, Sophie and Anna hadn't dared to ask again if they could play. Disappointed, they watched the boys. One day during recess, they approached one of the boys and asked, "We know the rules! Why can't we play with you?"

The boy looked at them as if Sophie and Anna were aliens. "You're girls…" he replied with a grin and walked away. Sophie was annoyed. "So what!" she exclaimed. This caught the attention of the other children. The boy continued to mock them. "Girls can't play soccer!" he sang. The other boys joined in, chanting, "Girls can't play soccer!"

By evening, they went home feeling sad. Sophie's father and mother tried to calm her down and encourage her. "That's not true. Girls can play soccer. And boys can play with dolls, too. It doesn't matter who you are — you can play whatever you want!"

Sophie agreed with her parents. She didn't understand why she wasn't allowed to play soccer. After all, she wasn't that different from the boys. She also had two feet and two legs to kick the ball. She had two hands to catch it as a goalkeeper. And she knew the rules. Why shouldn't she be able to play?

The next day, the girls were talking to each other.

"My dad and mom said we can play soccer!" said Sophie.

"I think so, too. There's nothing wrong with us being girls. Girls are allowed to play whatever they want!" added Anna.

"I think we should tell the boys that!" Sophie agreed.

"All right!" cheered Anna. Both of them were full of courage. But at the sidelines, their confidence faded. Instead, they watched the soccer game in silence. They didn't know how to start the conversation. They didn't know how to convince the boys. Day after day, week after week, recess passed without the girls saying a word to the boys.

But today, at the end of the break, it was too much. The boys called out, "Hey girls! Cheer us on properly for once, so we play better!" Sophie suddenly got angry.

"We don't want to cheer you on! We want to play, too!" she yelled.

"Oh, you're a girl. You wouldn't even know what to do with the ball!" one boy said.

Anna tried to defend Sophie. "Yes, we can play soccer! Our moms and dads said that girls can play soccer if they want to!" Sophie's outburst had caught the attention of a teacher. The teacher came over to the soccer field and asked what was going on.

"Kids, I heard shouting. What's happening?" the teacher asked.

Sophie, feeling guilty for yelling, looked down and said nothing. Anna, too shy, preferred to remain silent.

The boy complained to the teacher, clearly annoyed.

"Those two girls won't stop teasing us. And they won't cheer for us either!"

The teacher kindly replied, "If they don't want to cheer you on, that's their choice. Let them do what they want." Then, turning to the girls, the teacher asked, "Is it true that you're teasing the boys?"

Sophie raised her head and protested, "No, that's not true! We weren't teasing anyone! We just want to play soccer. They won't let us play! But my dad and mom said I could, even though I'm a girl!" Tears welled up in Sophie's eyes. She felt deeply wronged. She hadn't hurt anyone.

To the surprise of all the children, the teacher replied, "Your parents are absolutely right! You can play whatever you want. It doesn't matter if you're a girl or a boy. If you want to play soccer, then play soccer!"

One of the boys retorted, "No, but girls can't play soccer. They're bad, and I don't want them on our team."

The teacher asked him, "How do you

know girls are bad at soccer if you've never let them play?" This question made the boy pause. He didn't know what to say. Then, another boy suggested, "Fine. Let's let them play this time. Then everyone can see for themselves that they can't play well." He must have hoped that Sophie and Anna wouldn't dare, but he was wrong. Sophie and Anna joined

the game for the first time, glad to finally be part of it. They knew the rules and weren't clumsy with the ball. Sophie played especially well, passing the ball beautifully to her teammates and helping with some of the goals. Anna found herself a bit afraid of the ball, as people rushed at her whenever it came her way.

At the end of the game, Sophie and Anna's team had lost, but the teacher, who had been watching from afar, applauded them loudly.

"Bravo, Sophie! Bravo, Anna! That was your first game, and you did very well for beginners!" That was enough to put a big grin on the girls' faces. The boys on their team weren't happy about losing, but Sophie wasn't bothered.

"You'll see, if we keep practicing, we'll get even better!" she said confidently. If they played more often, she knew they would improve.

The boy who hadn't wanted them to play at first said, "You didn't do too badly. You can play again next time if you're on the other team."

Sophie and Anna agreed. They didn't really care which team they played on. As long as they could play soccer, they were happy.

It continued like that for several recesses. Sometimes they were on one team, sometimes the other. One day, they even won their first game. Anything is possible when you keep trying and believe you can do it.

The Swimming Pool

Julia was in a bad mood today. The bell rang for the first break, and she followed her classmates to play in the yard, but she seemed sad. She played without much motivation with Emilia and Mary, her two best friends. They were full of energy, running around with a ball they threw to each other. When the ball bounced against Julia's legs and stopped in front of her, Emilia and Mary became restless.

"Go on, Julia, shoot!" the two friends urged. With a sad expression, Julia kicked the ball to Emilia.

Recess ended with the ringing of the bell, reminding the children to line up in front of their classroom. Julia felt a knot in her stomach. She walked slowly, her head hanging low. Emilia and Mary wouldn't wait for her, both running eagerly to the classroom and shouting, "Go! Hurry up! We have swimming now!"

Emilia and Mary were looking forward to swimming. Julia, however, would have preferred any sport that didn't involve a bathing suit.

When Julia was a baby, she had been very sick. She'd spent a lot of time in hospitals, visiting doctors, and going to the pharmacy. One of her many health problems had required surgery. Because of that surgery, she now had a large scar on her right knee. Julia was so young when all of this happened that she couldn't even remember what kind of illness she had. Her parents had only told her it had been very complicated. Still, she was better now, and that was all that mattered. So, Julia never asked about her illness—only about her scar.

As far as she could remember, she always hated the strange mark on her leg. The skin felt uncomfortable and wasn't the same color as the rest of her body. "That scar is ugly," she told herself every day when she looked at her leg in the mirror. She never looked at it for very long because it disgusted her. She mostly wore long pants to hide it. Even for gym class, when all the other kids wore shorts, she would always cover her legs.

At school, no one had ever seen her scar, not even Emilia and Mary! Today that was going to change. They were going to the swimming pool for gym class, and even with a one-piece swimsuit, it was impossible to cover the scar. Everyone would see it. Everyone would be disgusted by her. No one would want to go near her anymore. No one would want to play with her.

Tears welled up in Julia's eyes, but she held them back as best she could.

Mom and Dad always told her, "You're beautiful just the way you are. Even your flaws are beautiful; they're what make you unique. If you can't love your scar, that's fine. The scar is only physical, and what matters is what's on the inside!" They said this while pointing to her chest, where her heart was.

Julia knew she was strong, and she would do anything not to cry. She would hang in there and find a way to hide her scar.

Julia got on the bus that took the whole class to the swimming pool. She let Mary and Emilia sit together and sat behind them. She didn't feel like arguing with anyone. She wanted to be left alone with her thoughts.

The moment they arrived, Julia's anxiety spiked. Her heart was beating loudly and fast. She felt incredibly nervous. She followed her classmates to the locker room, moving forward without really meaning to. It was as if she were caught in a nightmare.

Julia took a quick look around. The girls' locker room was quite large. The boys had their own locker room further down the hall. There were benches all along the walls with hooks to hang clothes on. There was no place to hide.

Fortunately, Julia spotted a large pillar at the end of the room and immediately stepped behind it. This way, she could at least hide from some of her classmates.

She put her things on the bench and looked around. Her classmates had hurried to take off their clothes and put

on their swimsuits, chatting excitedly.
Julia, still fully dressed, didn't move. She
felt lonely.

"I'm probably the only one with an ugly
scar," she thought. "The other girls all
look so happy and confident!" Tears
welled in her eyes.

One by one, the girls came out of the
locker room, each wrapped in towels to
keep warm while waiting to enter the
pool.

Even Mary and Emilia were already
outside. They were all waiting for Julia.
She sat down on the bench and waited.
"Maybe if I stay here and don't make any
noise, they'll forget about me. Then, I

won't have to go to the swimming pool!"
Julia thought, hopefully.

Unfortunately, her teacher quickly
noticed she was missing.
"Julia? Julia, where are you?" the teacher
called out.
Emilia informed her, "I don't know what
Julia is doing. She didn't change, and
she's still in the locker room!"

The teacher instructed the class to wait
by the pool. Then she strode into the
locker room. Opening the door slowly,
she called, "Julia?" letting her eyes scan
the room. At first, she couldn't see anyone
and started to feel anxious.

Julia hesitated for a moment, but when she realized how worried her teacher was, she weakly answered, "I'm here." The teacher was relieved and walked toward the pillar at the end of the room. She peered behind it and saw Julia sitting on the bench, still fully dressed, with tears in her eyes.

"Julia? Why aren't you wearing your swimsuit? Did you forget it at home?" the teacher asked kindly.
"No," Julia whispered, sulking. She almost wished she had forgotten it—that would've been the perfect excuse not to swim. Why hadn't she thought of it before?

The teacher sat down next to her, seeing that it would take a while. "Are you in pain? Are you feeling unwell?"

"No," Julia said again, this time so quietly she could barely be heard.

"Then talk to me, Julia. I can't guess what's wrong, so tell me," the teacher gently urged.

Julia began to cry. She wanted to explain but found it hard to talk about. Through her tears, she managed to say, "I … I … I don't want the other kids to see my ugly scar."

The teacher finally understood why Julia was so upset. She knew about Julia's illness and the surgeries but had never thought Julia might be ashamed of it.

"Oh, Julia, I'm so sorry! I didn't realize you'd feel embarrassed about swimming. I should've talked with you earlier!" Julia didn't answer, but she couldn't stop crying either.

"You know what, Julia? I don't think anyone will even notice your scar," the teacher said.
Julia didn't believe her and angrily replied, "Yes, they will! They'll look at it, and everyone will laugh. Then I won't have any friends left!"

"No, that's not true. Your classmates are too excited about swimming. No one will be paying attention to your scar!" Seeing that Julia was softening, the teacher continued, "And in the water, no one can see anything clearly anyway! Even those who swim with their eyes open underwater won't notice it."

"That's true!" Julia admitted. She had a small pool in her backyard during the summer, and she could never see much underwater.

"Also, always remember, Julia: your scar is a part of you. It's nothing to be ashamed of. You're beautiful just the way you are—scar or no scar!" the teacher added. Julia allowed herself to be convinced. She quickly changed, followed the teacher, and joined the rest of the group.

The teacher dodged the students' questions, saying simply, "We had a little problem, but everything's okay now. Are you all ready to swim?"
All the children shouted, "Yes!" with excitement.

For Julia, it was time to put aside the towel and expose her scar. She was still a little anxious, but she took a deep breath and bravely pulled the towel away.

She froze for a moment, looking around nervously, but no one was paying attention to her scar. She breathed a sigh of relief.

Suddenly, Emilia and Mary appeared in front of her.

"Julia, there you are!" Emilia said delightedly.

"We're finally going in the water!" Mary added, smiling happily.

Julia froze again. Her two friends were so close — they would surely see her scar. Then Mary's gaze fell on it.

"Oh, what happened to your knee? Did you fall?" she asked, simply curious.

Fighting back tears, Julia answered in a shaky voice, "No, it happened when I was little. I had surgery, and now my knee is ugly."

Emilia looked at the scar and said, "No, it's not ugly. You look like a brave warrior who fought in battle."

"Yeah! It looks just like in the movies. The heroes always have scars like that!" Mary added.

Impressed by her friends' reactions, Julia began to smile again.

Emilia, Mary, and Julia lined up at the edge of the pool, continuing to chat about the scar. Emilia and Mary kept saying how cool it was and how it made Julia special. Julia felt so much better, encouraged and supported by her friends.

Her teacher had been right: only her two best friends noticed the scar. The other children hadn't seen it at all. Calm, confident, and happy, Julia followed the teacher's instructions and jumped into the water with a light heart.

She would never be ashamed of her scar again.
She would never try to hide it again.
If anyone asked, she would proudly say, "I'm a warrior!"

I am perfect
the way I am

Math

Annabelle was in second grade and loved school. She loved playing with her friends in the schoolyard most of all, but she also enjoyed German and English classes. She loved learning new words and practicing her speaking skills.

"Hallo, ich heiße Annabelle," she said to everyone she met.

Today, she was waiting for the results of a math test. She felt anxious because math was always her weakest subject. She didn't like math, and it seemed that math didn't like her much either. No matter how hard she tried, she had never earned a good grade in that subject.

Still, she practiced her arithmetic! Sometimes, she spent more time on math than all her other subjects combined, yet it was never enough.

In class, the teacher announced, "It's time to give your papers back and correct them together!" Annabelle felt a knot forming in her stomach. She hoped for a miracle. She prayed to finally get a B in math, though deep down, she already knew she would probably receive another C.

The test had been on multiplication tables. She had to memorize all of them. She spent every evening, weekend, and even her last vacation studying. Still, the only multiplication table she could easily remember was the fives: five, ten, fifteen, twenty, and so on. That was child's play for her. But with the other numbers, Annabelle struggled.

The teacher walked through the rows, handing back each student's work. Sometimes, she made a little comment like, "Very nicely done," or, "Bravo, keep it up!" But when she reached Annabelle, the teacher said, "You need to study a little more."

Annabelle gasped. The teacher thought she didn't study? How awful! She was such a good student in all her other subjects. How could the teacher think, even for a moment, that Annabelle hadn't been diligent?

Annabelle quickly peeked at her grade. On her paper, she saw a big D written in red. She began to cry softly, feeling so sad and disappointed. A D! Worse than usual. After the teacher had handed back all the papers, she began to go over the answers on the board, but Annabelle couldn't focus. All she could think about was her grade and what the teacher had said.

After the last lesson ended, she left school and met her parents at the front gate. Mom and Dad immediately noticed their daughter looked upset.

"How are you, Annabelle? Did you have a nice day?" they asked.

Annabelle didn't answer. She got into the car and sulked all the way home.

Only when they were home did Annabelle decide to speak. She knew her parents wouldn't be mad, but they might be disappointed.

"I got my math grade today," she began quietly.

Mom and Dad exchanged a glance, now understanding what had happened. They knew Annabelle well and knew that math wasn't her strong suit.

"So, what grade did you get?" Dad asked kindly.

Annabelle burst into tears and told them she had gotten a D. She was heartbroken.

All that work, all that effort, and for nothing. Mom and Dad took Annabelle in their arms and tried to comfort her. The only thing she could say through her sobs was,

"It's not fair! I studied so hard for this test!" Her parents knew she had prepared diligently. They had watched her. They had even tried to help. But the day before the test, they had noticed that Annabelle had barely memorized anything.

Mom and Dad felt very sorry for her. She had done her best, and it was heartbreaking to see her like this. They tried everything to cheer her up.

"It's okay, Annabelle. It's only one grade. I'm sure the next one will be better," Mom said.

"You have good grades in your other

subjects. Maybe languages just suit you more," Dad added.

That evening, Annabelle went to bed early, exhausted from her difficult day. Mom and Dad's words kept buzzing around in her head:
"It's not bad,"
"You did your best, and that's the main thing,"
"Don't get discouraged, you'll do better next time." Finally, Annabelle fell asleep.

When she woke up, she already felt a little better. It seemed that she had absorbed her parents' encouragement overnight. At breakfast, Annabelle's parents tried to boost her confidence again.

"Did you know your dad was bad at English in school?" Mom said with a mischievous look.

Annabelle looked at her in amazement. "That can't be! Dad is so smart!" Then Dad joined in,
"Maybe I'm smart, but I was bad at English back then. Did you know that your mom wasn't good at math?" Annabelle laughed. "No way! Mom is great at math!" She was convinced they were just teasing her.

"No, it's true, Annabelle," Mom replied, quietly but seriously.
"At school, there were subjects I didn't like at all. Sometimes, I studied so hard

and still got bad grades. Then, I was just as sad as you are now."

Dad added, "You can't be good at everything, and no one is perfect. Mom and I aren't perfect, either. And that's not a bad thing. We were good in some subjects and not in others. Everyone has strengths and weaknesses. That's what makes us special!"

Annabelle thought about their words. "That's true. Lea isn't good at sports. And Ben isn't good at German. He never understands anything, and I always have to explain it to him!" she said.

Mom smiled.

"See? It's the same for everyone. We all have our strengths and weaknesses. There's nothing wrong with that."

Annabelle finally understood what her parents meant, and her mood improved.

When Mom dropped her off at school, she said,
"Do you know that you're a very special girl? You're perfect just the way you are. No grade in the world will change that! Grades don't define a person's worth. It's okay if you have bad grades sometimes, and it's okay if there are subjects you don't like. The most important thing is that you always try your best."

Annabelle smiled.

"Yes, Mom. I'll keep doing my best.
And it's okay if I don't always get
good grades!" Yesterday's bad grade
was already becoming just a distant
memory. Annabelle started that day
with determination and newfound self-
confidence.

Never again would Annabelle cry over a bad grade. She would do her best and accept that not everything would always go perfectly.

I am
loved

Imprint

You Are Amazing, Girl
Megan Donovan
ISBN: 9798345299333
1st edition 2022
Responsible for printing: Amazon
Year of publication: 2nd Edition 2024

Made in the USA
Coppell, TX
24 November 2024

40949039R00062